Irish
Americans

Michael V. Uschan

Curriculum Consultant: Michael Koren,
Social Studies Teacher, Maple Dale School, Fox Point, Wisconsin

WORLD ALMANAC® LIBRARY

To Tom and Maggie Blaha—"May the wind be always at your back."

Please visit our web site at: www.garethstevens.com
For a free color catalog describing World Almanac® Library's
list of high-quality books and multimedia programs,
call 1-800-848-2928 (USA) or 1-800-387-3178 (Canada).
World Almanac® Library's fax: (414) 332-3567.

Library of Congress Cataloging-in-Publication Data

Uschan, Michael V., 1948-
    Irish Americans / by Michael V. Uschan.
       p. cm. — (World Almanac Library of American immigration)
    Includes bibliographical references and index.
    ISBN-10: 0-8368-7311-4 — ISBN-13: 978-0-8368-7311-5 (lib. bdg.)
    ISBN-10: 0-8368-7324-6 — ISBN-13: 978-0-8368-7324-5 (softcover)
    1. Irish Americans—History—Juvenile literature. 2. Immigrants—
United States—History—Juvenile literature. 3. United States—Emigration
and immigration—History—Juvenile literature. I. Title. II. Series.
    E184.I6U83   2006
    973'.049162—dc22   2006005320

First published in 2007 by
World Almanac® Library
A member of the WRC Media Family of Companies
330 West Olive Street, Suite 100
Milwaukee, WI 53212, USA

Copyright © 2007 by World Almanac® Library.

Produced by Discovery Books
Editor: Sabrina Crewe
Designer and page production: Sabine Beaupré
Photo researcher: Sabrina Crewe
Maps and diagrams: Stefan Chabluk
Consultant: Andy Urban
World Almanac® Library editorial direction: Mark J. Sachner
World Almanac® Library editor: Barbara Kiely Miller
World Almanac® Library art direction: Tammy West
World Almanac® Library production: Jessica Morris

Picture credits: Collections of the New York Public Library, Astor, Lenox and Tilden
Foundations: 15; CORBIS: cover, 5, 21, 24, 38, 41, 43; Granger Collection: 9, 13, 23;
Library of Congress: title page, 7, 10, 11, 12, 18, 19, 22, 25, 26, 27, 28 (both), 29,
30 (both), 31, 32, 33, 34, 35, 36, 37, 42; National Park Service: 14.

Printed in the United States of America

1 2 3 4 5 6 7 8 9 10 09 08 07 06

Contents

Front cover: An Irish American police officer directs traffic in New York City in the 1930s. Since the late 1800s, Irish Americans have been prominent in U.S. police forces.

Title page: Photographed in Roxbury, Massachusetts, in 1912, the O'Donovan children (ages thirteen, eleven, nine, seven, and twins of four years old) worked tying tags to earn income for their family. In the late 1800s and early 1900s, many Irish American children worked instead of going to school.

Introduction

The United States has often been called "a nation of immigrants." With the exception of Native Americans—who have inhabited North America for thousands of years—all Americans can trace their roots to other parts of the world.

Immigration is not a thing of the past. More than seventy million people came to the United States between 1820 and 2005. One-fifth of that total—about fourteen million people—immigrated since the start of 1990. Overall, more people have immigrated permanently to the United States than to any other single nation.

Push and Pull

Historians write of the "push" and "pull" factors that lead people to emigrate. "Push" factors are the conditions in the homeland that convince people to leave. Many immigrants to the United States were—and still are—fleeing persecution or poverty. "Pull" factors are those that attract people to settle in another country. The dream of freedom or jobs or both continues to pull immigrants to the United States. People from many countries around the world view the United States as a place of opportunity.

Building a Nation

Immigrants to the United States have not always found what they expected. People worked long hours for little pay, often

"There was nothing subtle about their dreams—they [Irish immigrants] had come to this land so that their children could enjoy a better life. Our ancestors were the survivors of oppression and famine, those desperate enough to seek refuge in steerage. But when their spirit burst forth upon this great land of the United States, they and the nation prospered."

Kevin M. Cahill, President-General of the American Irish Historical Society, 2005

▲ This print from about 1870 shows a St. Patrick's Day parade in Union Square, New York City. Irish Americans have celebrated St. Patrick's Day since the 1700s.

doing jobs that others did not want to do. Many groups also endured prejudice.

In spite of these challenges, immigrants and their children built the United States of America, from its farms, railroads, and computer industries to its beliefs and traditions. They have enriched American life with their culture and ideas. Although they honor their heritage, most immigrants and their descendants are proud to call themselves Americans first and foremost.

The Irish Americans

In 1607, Irishman Francis Magnel was among the settlers who arrived in North America and founded the colony of Jamestown, Virginia. In the four centuries since then, more than seven million Irish people have come to the United States. In 2004, more than thirty-four million Americans—or about 12 percent of the U.S. population—claimed Irish heritage. The population of Ireland itself, meanwhile, stands at fewer than four million people.

For nearly a century, many other Americans discriminated against Irish Americans for two reasons: their Irish ancestry and their Roman Catholic religion. Irish Americans fought and overcame such prejudice and went on to make many important contributions to the United States. Irish Americans used their literary skills to enhance U.S. poetry, plays, and novels, while the strong traditions of Irish folk music found their way into American popular music.

Life in the Homeland

I n Gaelic, the ancient language of Ireland, the country is known as Eire. The Gaelic language was brought to Ireland in about 400 B.C. by Celtic tribes from Europe.

Centuries of Invasion

The Celts were the first of three groups that invaded Ireland, dominated the native population, and profoundly changed the island. In the ninth century, Viking raiders from Denmark and Norway began raiding Ireland. Many Vikings eventually settled in Ireland and established several cities, including Dublin, Cork, Limerick, and Waterford.

The most significant invasion came in 1171,

◀ Ireland is an island near the coast of Europe. Most of the island forms the Republic of Ireland. Northern Ireland—sometimes known as Ulster because historically that was the name for the northeastern region—is part of the United Kingdom of Great Britain (which also includes England, Wales, and Scotland). Ireland is divided into counties, and some cities bear the same name as the counties in which they are located.

◀ Irish peasants lived in tiny, dark cottages, where they struggled to survive. This woman in County Donegal was photographed in about 1900 spinning wool in her cottage.

when King Henry II of England conquered Ireland and seized most of the land. He gave the land to English nobles and allowed them to govern Ireland. Over time, the families of these nobles and of local Gaelic-speaking leaders combined to rule over the poorer people of Ireland, who farmed the land and served the landowners.

Persecution of Catholics

In 1534, British king Henry VIII separated his kingdom from the Roman Catholic Church to form the Church of England. In 1603, to weaken Catholic influence, King James I seized Irish land in the northern province of Ulster and gave it to Protestants from England and Scotland. Some descendants of those Scots emigrated and became known in America as the Scotch-Irish, or Scots-Irish.

In the 1600s, the British introduced Penal Laws that stripped the Irish of basic rights. Catholic churches were closed, and Catholics could not buy land, attend school, vote, or speak Gaelic. Most of these harsh laws existed until 1829. Despite the persecution and restrictions, the Irish remained fiercely loyal to their faith.

Life under British Rule

By the 1800s, long-term discrimination in favor of Protestants had reduced most Irish Catholics to peasants—poor farmers who grew wheat, barley, and potatoes on a few acres of land they rented from English landowners. Their houses were small and made of dried mud or stone with a grass roof. To heat their homes and cook food,

Irish peasants burned chunks of dried peat, the thick layers of decayed plant matter cut from the bogs, or wetlands, which covered great areas of Ireland.

Although the Penal Laws outlawed Catholic education, some Catholic children learned to read and write in "hedge schools." These were illegal schools hidden behind hedges or in other places. The few Catholics who could still afford to do so sent their children to other countries to become educated.

Even the Scottish community in Ulster suffered from discrimination. Because they were Presbyterian—a Protestant denomination separate from the Church of England—the English applied some Penal Laws against them. This angered the Presbyterians because, like Catholics, they believed their own faith was the true one.

Reasons to Leave

Harsh living conditions, combined with religious discrimination and a lack of social and political freedom, led many Irish to leave for

Community Life

The difficult conditions of their daily existence made it important for the Irish to find a way to bring some joy into their lives. The most important way they did this was through socializing in big groups at weddings, feast days for Catholic saints, and other holidays. They even did this at wakes, the traditional gatherings held in Ireland when someone died.

On special occasions, everyone for miles around was invited to a celebration that always included music and dancing. The Irish played tunes on instruments that included the violin, flute, tin whistle, harp, and bagpipes. They performed many type of dances including step dancing, which involved intricate kicks and turns and was often performed in a group. Couples and individuals did reels, jigs, and even polkas, a dance that came from Europe.

Young men might compete in hurling, an ancient sport that was once used to train Irish warriors for battle. Players wield a curved wooden stick called a hurley to hit, pass, and carry a ball over a large grassy field. It can be a rough game because opponents try to stop one another from advancing the ball.

The food served at celebrations was simple. The main source of food for the Irish was the potato, the cheapest nutritious food available. Their diet was supplemented by a few other vegetables and, on special occasions, a small amount of meat, but potatoes were usually all that Irish peasants ate daily.

the British colonies in North America during the 1700s. These people —many of them tradesmen, skilled workers, or other professionals— hoped to find religious freedom and the opportunity to own land. Most of them were Protestants, and many were the Scotch-Irish whose ancestors had settled in the northern province of Ulster.

In 1798, a group of Catholics, Presbyterian, and Episcopalian Irish joined together to try and gain Ireland's independence from British rule. Led by Theobald Wolfe Tone, the uprising of the United Irishmen failed when it was crushed by British troops. Many of the United Irishmen fled Ireland to Philadelphia, Pennsylvania, where they became active in U.S. politics.

By the early 1800s, many Irish Catholics were deciding to leave their homeland. Most were peasant farmers and unskilled workers hoping to escape the terrible poverty of their existence in Ireland. Emigrants of the 1800s included more families and single women than those who had left Ireland in earlier years.

The Great Famine

In 1845, farmers in Ireland expected a bumper crop of potatoes because the summer had been wet, which was good for growing. Before they could be harvested, however, a blight withered and blackened the potatoes, destroying three-fourths of the nation's crop. Potatoes were the main source of food for the Irish poor. A story in the *Spectator* newspaper summed up the disaster that was beginning to unfold: "Whole fields of the root have rotted in the ground, and many a family sees its sole provision for the year destroyed."

The potato blight created the darkest period in Irish history, known as

▶ A starving mother and her child search a field, hoping to find potatoes that have survived the blight during the Great Famine.

▲ The city of Galway, shown here in about 1900, is one of Ireland's ancient towns. By the time this photograph was taken, death and mass emigration had reduced Ireland's population by nearly half.

the Great Famine or *an Gorta Mor* (Gaelic for the Great Hunger). The blight returned yearly through 1851, reducing Ireland's annual potato yield to 20 percent of normal. In those six years, nearly one million people starved to death or died of diseases associated with inadequate diet. One illness was typhus, which was nicknamed "road fever" because the bodies of so many of its victims littered roads throughout Ireland. The first recorded death occurred in Skibbereen, a community that became linked forever to the horror the famine caused.

The potato blight devastated the Irish people. In addition to creating starvation by denying them their main source of food, it left people penniless because they had no potatoes to sell. As a result, British landlords evicted a half-million people from their homes because they could not pay rent. These same landlords, meanwhile, continued to export the products of Irish labor. Meat, dairy products, and grain—the very food that could have saved the starving Irish—was sent to England.

The famine reached its peak in 1847. That year, Bridget Nolan of County Kilkenny wrote her son, who had emigrated to Rhode Island in the United States: "This is the poorest winter that ever I had since I began the world, without house nor home nor a bit of food to eat." Nolan's husband had died and she had been evicted. She was one of millions of Irish people who suffered, starved, and died before the blight finally went away.

"Oh, son! I loved my native land with energy and pride,
Till a blight came o'er my crops—my sheep, my cattle died;
My rent and taxes were too high, I could not them redeem,
And that's the cruel reason that I left old Skibbereen."

From a song by an unknown writer in the mid-1800s about the Great Famine that drove him out of Ireland

Fleeing Ireland

Bridget Nolan's son, on the other hand, was one of hundreds of thousands of people who fled to the United States during the famine years. The Irish who left their country to escape death in the famine, however, never forgot the role the British had played in the starvation and oppression of their people.

The Great Famine was the main reason for leaving Ireland, but the Irish continued to emigrate in large numbers for many years after the famine ended. They left largely because they had little opportunity to own land and make a living under British rule.

Independence

In 1922, everything changed with creation of the Irish Free State. Northern Ireland, with its large Protestant population, remained under British rule, but the rest of Ireland had finally won its independence from Britain.

In the 1930s, people stopped emigrating from Ireland in such large numbers. Conflict with the British continued as groups in Ireland fought for control of Northern Ireland. In spite of these struggles, the Irish found fewer reasons to leave their homeland. The nation's economy improved dramatically in the 1960s and 1970s and again in recent years. Today, fewer than two thousand people are leaving Ireland for the United States each year.

"[In a home were] six famished and ghastly skeletons, to all appearances dead, huddled in a corner on some filthy straw. I approached in horror and found by a low moaning they were alive. They were in a fever—four children, a woman, and what had once been a man."

Nicholas Cummins, a government official from County Cork, on an inspection tour of an Irish village in 1846

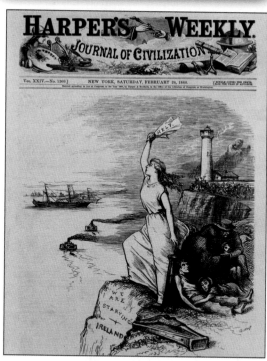

▲ A magazine illustration shows a woman with her harp beside her, representing Ireland, standing next to starving Irish people. Called "The Herald of Relief from America," the drawing shows ships carrying food sent by Irish Americans and others in the United States during a famine in 1880.

CHAPTER 2

Emigration

There is no Gaelic word to describe the act of leaving Ireland voluntarily. Instead, the Gaelic term usually used for immigration is *deorai*, which means exile, or forced departure. Many Irish felt they were forced to leave their beloved homeland. Others, however, especially women, saw emigration as an opportunity for independence and a way of escaping the constraints of Irish society.

From a Stream to a Tidal Wave

Millions of Irish people left a homeland they loved and braved the dangers of a long journey for one reason—to have a better life. Many of them had first learned of the promise of this new life in what became known as "America letters" that other immigrants sent home. In 1818, John Doyle was living in New York City and working to make money to pay his wife's passage to the United States.

In a letter to her, Doyle praised his new homeland: "There is a great many inconveniences here but no empty bellies."

Between 1600 and 1776 (when the American colonies declared their independence from Britain), an estimated 250,000 people

◀ A photograph taken in the early 1900s shows two women outside an Irish cottage, one reading to the other a letter that has arrived from the United States. Over the years, letters such as this encouraged growing numbers of Irish people to join family and friends who had already emigrated.

▲ In a County Kerry town, people gather around a mail coach that will carry emigrants to the nearest port. There, the emigrants will start their sea journey, first to England and then to the United States.

emigrated from Ireland to North America. Many more came as the years passed. Between 1831 and 1840, more than 200,000 Irish—most of them men—emigrated from Ireland to the United States.

The Great Famine that began in 1845 turned the steady stream of emigrants into a tidal wave. More than 900,000 fled to the United States in the 1850s. These emigrants were mostly families. During the next thirty years, an average of 500,000 Irish people emigrated to the United States each decade. After the famine ended, not as many families left. The typical emigrant was instead young and single and, increasingly, female.

After 1890, emigration declined, slowly at first and then dramatically when Ireland became independent in the 1920s. In recent years, the only decade in which more than 50,000 Irish emigrated to the United States was 1991–2000. In those years, Ireland's economy was struggling, and people left hoping to find better jobs.

Leaving Home

Deorai was heartbreaking for people left behind as well as for those moving to the United States. Diarmuid O'Donovan Rossa describes the farewell in 1848 when his mother, brother, and sister left Skibbereen with other emigrants: "The cry of the weeping and wailing of that day rings in my ears still. [It] was a cry heard every day in Ireland." A few years later, Rossa also moved to the United States.

During the peak years of Irish emigration to the United States, the 3,000-mile (4,800-kilometer) voyage across the Atlantic Ocean to the United States usually began in the large port of Liverpool, England, and ended in the U.S. cities of New York, Philadelphia, Boston, or New Orleans. Irish emigrants first had to leave their villages and travel to an Irish port, then cross the Irish Sea to England and make their way to Liverpool. There, they went through a medical inspection. Many emigrants, especially during the Great Famine, were sick from malnutrition or disease, and they could be refused passage.

The Coffin Ships

The ocean voyage was long and dangerous. The sailing ships that traveled the ocean until the late 1800s often took three months to make the crossing. Voyages on these ships were a nightmare because of overcrowding, lack of food, and unsanitary conditions.

▲ A steamship company poster advertises weekly departures from Liverpool to New York City. The poster offers comfortable cabins in "saloon passage" and cheap fares in steerage.

Some passengers could afford a private room with a bed. Most were so poor, however, that they had to travel in steerage, an area below decks that usually held cargo. Hundreds of people were crowded together in this dirty, cramped space along with their possessions, including pigs and other animals. Their beds were rows of wooden boards nailed to the sides of the ships. Their toilets were buckets that were emptied once a day.

The shipping company was supposed to provide food and cooking facilities, but these were rarely sufficient. Passengers often brought their own food, usually hard oatcakes. Water and food were always in short supply and often ran out before the trip ended, or it

▲ Steerage accommodation was crowded, dirty, and uncomfortable. Passengers who emigrated before the days of steamship travel spent months cooped up below deck, where diseases spread easily and many people died.

became spoiled or contaminated by filthy conditions. "The steerage was a dirty place [and] the food ran scarce," is the way Ann McNabb described her trip in the mid-1800s aboard the *Mary Jane*.

"Hundreds of poor people, men, women, and children, of all ages from the driveling idiot of ninety to the babe just born, are huddled together without light, without air, wallowing in filth and breathing a fetid atmosphere, sick in body, dispirited in heart. . . . The food was seldom sufficiently cooked because there was not enough opportunities for drinking and cooking. Washing was impossible; and in many ships the filthy beds were never brought up on deck and aired, nor was the narrow space between the sleeping berths washed or scraped until arrival."

Irish emigrant Stephen DeVere who traveled to the United States during the Great Famine

In spite of the medical inspections in Liverpool, many of the Irish traveling to the United States were sick and starving when they boarded the ships. So many passengers died that the vessels became known as "coffin ships." In 1847 alone, nearly 17,500 Irish emigrants died during the voyage across the Atlantic Ocean.

Later Travelers

Toward the end of the 1800s, steam-powered ships replaced sailing ships. The more modern ships made the crossing in a week to ten days. Emigrants continued to travel by ship up to the 1950s, when airplanes began to carry people from Ireland to the United States. The journey became much easier, but the challenges of arrival in a new country still had to be faced.

CHAPTER 3

Arriving in the United States

The earliest Irish immigrants were often too poor to pay for their passage from Ireland. When the ships carrying these people to North America arrived, they were met by employers who were prepared to pay a passenger's fare in return for a promise of work. This system was known as indentured servitude, and many Irish and British immigrants arrived in colonial America as indentured servants.

Indentured Servants

An indentured servant had to work for the employer for several years to repay the money for the fare. Many Irish immigrants lived harsh lives in conditions similar to slavery. Once their servitude was over, however, they were free to pursue opportunities they would never have had in Ireland.

Charles Thomson was indentured when he arrived in Philadelphia, Pennsylvania, in 1739 as a ten-year-old orphan. Like other children, he had to work for the person who purchased his services until he was an adult. After being freed from service, Thomson became a rich Philadelphia merchant and a leader in the American Revolution.

Settling the Colonies

Many Irish immigrants went to northern cities, such as Philadelphia and New

"It appeared that a trade was carried on in human flesh between Pennsylvania and the province of Ulster. When they [indentured servants] are brought to Philadelphia, they are either sold aboard the vessel, or by public [auction]. They bring generally about fifteen pounds currency at market, are sold for the terms of their indentures, which is from two to four years, and on its expiration, receive a suit of clothes, and implements of husbandry [farming], consisting of a hoe, an axe, and a bill from their taskmasters [setting them free]."

Letter from a Dr. Williams to the Belfast News, *an Irish newspaper, March 22, 1774*

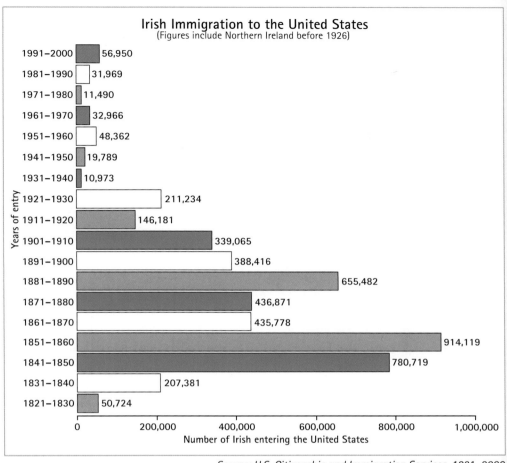

Irish Immigration to the United States
(Figures include Northern Ireland before 1926)

Years of entry	Number
1991–2000	56,950
1981–1990	31,969
1971–1980	11,490
1961–1970	32,966
1951–1960	48,362
1941–1950	19,789
1931–1940	10,973
1921–1930	211,234
1911–1920	146,181
1901–1910	339,065
1891–1900	388,416
1881–1890	655,482
1871–1880	436,871
1861–1870	435,778
1851–1860	914,119
1841–1850	780,719
1831–1840	207,381
1821–1830	50,724

Number of Irish entering the United States

Source: U.S. Citizenship and Immigration Services, 1821–2000

▲ This chart shows how many Irish people immigrated to the United States each decade since 1820. It is clear to see how immigration increased during the famine of 1845–1851 and decreased after U.S. immigration limits were imposed in 1924.

York, while others settled in less populated southern areas, such as South Carolina. Of the Catholics who arrived in colonial times, many made their way to Maryland. Lord Baltimore, an English Catholic noble, had established the colony in 1632 as a religious haven for English Catholics.

In the 1600s and 1700s, many Irish immigrants—most of them Scotch-Irish—became farmers. They moved to rural areas in Pennsylvania, Virginia, and North and South Carolina, where white settlement was just beginning.

Arriving in the Cities

By the 1800s, the vast majority of Irish immigrants were poor Catholics. At first, when these immigrants arrived in ports such

▲ Immigrants at Ellis Island in the early 1900s prepare to enter the United States and begin a new life. Before the immigration station closed in 1954, an estimated twelve to sixteen million immigrants passed through Ellis Island.

as Boston and New York City, they simply walked off their ships and began looking for work and a place to live. U.S. officials did not start recording their names until 1820, when they began to copy names from passenger lists of ships arriving in the United States. By the middle of the 1800s, however, so many new immigrants were arriving that the United States began opening offices to process them on arrival.

The first immigration station was Castle Garden, which opened August 1, 1855, in New York City. In a book that he wrote for immigrants in the 1870s, Father Stephen Byrne claimed the center was "essentially an institution of protection to the immigrant." The Catholic priest said officials provided immigrants with temporary accommodations, helped them travel to other cities, and exchanged gold, silver, or foreign money they carried for U.S. currency.

In 1892, the federal government opened twenty-four even larger immigration stations in cities that included New York, Baltimore, Boston, Seattle, San Francisco, and New Orleans. At these centers, officials examined immigrants for medical and mental problems that might make them unfit to enter the United States.

The Ellis Island Experience

Ellis Island in New York was the nation's busiest immigration station and the one that received the most Irish immigrants. Passengers who had been rich enough to afford their own cabins were given brief medical examinations on board their ships and

The First Arrival at Ellis Island

When fifteen-year-old Annie Moore came to the United States on January 1, 1892, she was more royally welcomed than any Irish immigrant had ever been. On that cold New Year's Day, Moore was selected by officials to be the first arrival at Ellis Island in New York City on its first day of operation. The young Irish girl was greeted by Charles M. Hendley of the U.S. Treasury, who gave her a $10 gold coin in honor of her historic arrival. More important to Moore than the gold coin, however, was the reunion she and her two younger brothers soon had with their parents, who were already living in New York.

▶ A photograph from about 1911 shows a woman undergoing a medical examination at Ellis Island. Medical officers looked out for infectious eye diseases such as trachoma, which causes blindness.

then allowed to enter the country. Immigrants who traveled in steerage were sent to Ellis Island for longer, more detailed inspections.

The first step in the process was to check immigrants' identification papers so officials could register their names. After their names were recorded, immigrants waited in long lines for a series of medical examinations. Medical officers checked for physical disabilities, mental illness, and contagious diseases such as tuberculosis. If medical officers were uncertain about someone's health, they could hold the person for several days to continue the medical examination. The process of being poked and prodded and examined in many other ways was intimidating for immigrants.

"Understaffed. Overcrowded. Jammed. And the place was the noisiest and the languages and the smell [were terrible],"

Emmanuel Steen, who arrived at Ellis Island from Dublin, Ireland, in 1925

Because the United States only wanted to admit healthy people, immigrants with serious medical problems were not allowed into

Becoming U.S. Citizens

Irish Americans have almost always had the right to become U.S. citizens. Before 1790, any white immigrant was considered a citizen. That year, however, U.S. Congress passed a law requiring people to live in the United States for two years before they could become citizens, in a process called naturalization. In 1795, Congress lengthened the waiting period to five years. To become a citizen today, immigrants to the United States must be of "good moral character," pass a test on U.S. history and government, and understand English. Children born in the United States of Irish American parents are automatically U.S. citizens.

the country. These travelers were given free passage back to their native countries. Although only about 2 percent of immigrants were denied entry, this practice of sending people back often divided families. If a father or mother was turned down, however, the whole family sometimes returned home.

After 1917, people could also be rejected if they were illiterate. The U.S. Congress passed a law that year requiring immigrants to be able to read or write. Immigrants could also be sent home if they were penniless or if they did not have any friends or relatives in the United States who could take responsibility for them.

First Impressions

The United States was a strange, new land to Irish immigrants. Most of them had come from rural areas or small towns, and the large U.S. cities that became their homes overwhelmed them. Even the Americans who would become their neighbors and friends seemed different. When Thomas Cather arrived in New York in 1836, he was astounded at how many people there were and how everyone rushed around at full speed. "The Americans appear to be a locomotive people," he observed. "There is always a crowd in motion."

When Josephine Cassidy arrived in Newark, New Jersey, she was amazed by large buildings that towered above her. "I had never seen them before," she said. Like other Irish immigrants, she had never been to a city that had buildings taller than a few stories. This new world also included foods, such as bananas, that many Irish people had never seen and didn't know how to eat.

▲ The Irish Emigrant Society was founded in 1841 by Irish Americans concerned about the welfare of new arrivals from their homeland. The society offered advice and help with work and accommodation. A bank opened by the society in 1850 offered Irish Americans a safe way to send money back to family members in Ireland.

For immigrants, the strangeness of their new home was often softened by the presence of other Irish people. The vast majority of the Irish Catholics that came in the 1800s chose to settle in large cities, including Boston, Chicago, Pittsburgh, and New York, where Irish communities quickly developed.

"New York is a grand handsome city. But you would hardly know you had left Ireland, there are so many Irish people here. Some of them are become rich. Some of them are big men in government. For most of us it is hard work, but there is plenty of it and the pay is all right. . . . Soon I will send you some money I have saved. I know that will help you and you will not feel so bad about how I had to leave you."

Irish immigrant Patrick Murphy in a letter to his mother in Ireland, September 15, 1885

War, Poverty, and Prejudice

I rish Americans played a significant role in creating and building the United States. They not only helped settle the first British colonies, but they fought to help their adopted homeland win its independence from Britain in the American Revolution. Irish Americans also provided much of the muscle that helped the young country expand in its first few decades as a nation. In the 1820s, a journalist wrote: "There are several kinds of power working at the fabric of the republic—water-power, steam-power, and Irish power. The last works hardest of all."

Colonial Irish Americans

In the 1600s and 1700s, Irish immigration to the American colonies, mostly by Protestants, was second only to that of the English. Although most became farmers, like other colonists, some

Irish Americans had other skills, such as glassmaking, that helped them find work and prosper in their new homeland.

Irish Americans helped settle New York, Pennsylvania, and Virginia. Then they began traveling south through Virginia's Shenandoah Valley to the newer

◄ In 1769, Irish American Daniel Boone led settlers into the region that would eventually become the state of Kentucky. Six years later, he founded Boonesborough, Kentucky's first permanent white settlement.

colonies of North and South Carolina. One of those adventurous Irish Americans was the legendary Daniel Boone, who explored several unmapped regions of North America.

Fighting for Independence

When the American Revolution began in 1775, Irish Americans joyously fought the British, perhaps in retaliation for the way the British had treated the Irish. One-third to one-half of the soldiers in the Continental Army were Irish, including twenty-six generals. They fought so well and so bravely that British politician Lord Mountjoy claimed, "We have lost America through the Irish."

Irish Americans also helped form the political principles that are the foundation of U.S. government. In 1776, nine Irish American

▲ Charles Carroll of Carrollton

The Carroll Family

Not all Irish immigrants were poor. Charles Carroll (1661–1720) was descended from a formerly rich and powerful Irish Catholic family that, like others, had been persecuted by English Protestants in Ireland. In 1688, Carroll arrived in the Catholic colony of Maryland.

Although the Catholics soon lost their power in the colony, Carroll prospered, building the largest estate in the colony. His son, also named Charles (1702–1782), expanded that estate to become a hugely wealthy landowner and slave owner. It was the third Charles—Charles Carroll of Carrollton (1713–1832)—who took a different route by becoming a leader in the struggle for independence during the American Revolution. Carroll (said by some historians to be the richest man in America at the time) was the only Catholic to sign the Declaration of Independence. Charles Carroll had two distinguished cousins. Daniel Carroll (1730–1796), another rich landowner and Revolutionary leader, was one of only two Catholics to sign the U.S. Constitution. Daniel's brother John (1735–1815) was appointed the first Catholic bishop of the United States of America in 1789.

members of the Continental Congress approved and signed the Declaration of Independence.

Moving West

In the 1820s, mountain men such as Thomas Fitzpatrick, an Irish immigrant who was a part owner of the Rocky Mountain Fur Company, began trapping beaver in the far west of North America, exploring the region that was little known to white Americans. The mountain men followed Native American trails to California and Oregon, developing routes that were later used by white settlers.

When gold was discovered in California in 1848, tens of thousands of people moved west to search for riches. Among them was Jeremiah O'Sullivan, who in 1859 found silver in Virginia City, Nevada. In a letter to his brother in Ireland, O'Sullivan wrote that he and a companion had "struck a vein of purest silver, and are in the prospect of becoming very rich men."

Irish American Farmers

Unlike earlier arrivals, only a small minority of Irish immigrants in the 1800s became farmers. Catholic Bishop John Lancaster Spalding wrote in his 1880 history of Irish Americans that only about 8 percent of them took up farming. He claimed that this percentage was smaller than for any other immigrant group. In 1885, however, farmer John R. Reily wrote that he preferred rural life because there was less religious prejudice: "It is easier to be a Catholic here than in the mixed and busy push of towns and cities." He lived in Conewago, an Irish Catholic community near present-day Altoona, Pennsylvania. The farming

◄ An 1882 photograph shows Irish clam diggers on a wharf in Boston, Massachusetts, one of the main northeastern cities in which Irish Americans settled. Clam digging was traditionally an Irish American occupation in New England.

community had been founded by Michael McGuire, who had been an army officer during the American Revolution.

Prejudice in the Cities

Most Irish immigrants were too poor to buy land and become farmers. In addition, farms required whole families to work them, and many Irish came to America alone. So they settled in the cities where they found work and the support of existing Irish American communities. By the 1800s, most Irish Americans lived and worked in these large cities, and new immigrants poured in every month.

Up until the middle of the nineteenth century, Americans had accepted Irish immigrants. In 1828, Andrew Jackson, the son of Scotch-Irish immigrants, was elected president. At the same time, however, many Americans were turning against Irish Americans.

The main reason for this prejudice was that more recent immigrants were Roman Catholics. The majority of Irish Americans who arrived before 1800 had been Protestant, like most other white Americans of the period. As Catholic immigration increased, anti-Catholic feeling sometimes flared into violence. In Philadelphia in 1844, nativists burned down several churches and killed thirteen

⌃ An 1852 advertisement for the nativist newspaper *American Patriot* uses anti-Catholic images to express its views that immigration, especially by Irish Catholics, would be the ruin of U.S. society and institutions.

Catholics. They had been angry that Irish Catholic schools were teaching the Catholic Bible instead of the Protestant version.

The newer Irish immigrants were also less welcome because they were poorer, less educated, and had fewer job skills than earlier arrivals. By 1850, Joseph Brennan claimed in a letter to his family in Dublin that the Irish were now "shunned and despised," and their situation was "one of shame and poverty." Brennan pointed out that the growing prejudice against the Irish had "crossed the Atlantic with our people." Most Americans who discriminated against the Irish were descendants of English Protestant immigrants, the same group that had persecuted Irish Catholics in Ireland. Many Anglo Americans viewed the "Irish race" as somewhere between whites and blacks and treated them accordingly. Irish Americans struggled hard to be treated as "white," and this challenge made many of them prejudiced against blacks, Asians, and other ethnic minorities as they tried to gain acceptance for themselves.

▲ A 1941 photo shows the chimneys of textile mills towering over the town of Lowell, Massachusetts, where generations of immigrants performed grueling work in the 1800s and early 1900s. Many of the earliest immigrants to arrive in Lowell were Irish, and soon Irish American neighborhoods formed around the mills.

"No Irish Need Apply"

The most damaging discrimination Irish Americans faced was in getting work. The hateful phrase "No Irish Need Apply" sometimes accompanied advertisements for job openings. For much of the 1800s, most Irish Americans could get only the hardest, lowest-paying jobs because so many employers refused to hire them for better jobs. Even skilled workers, such as carpenters, could not get good jobs.

Hard Work, Low Pay

In 1855, 20 percent of Irish Americans in New York City were classified as unskilled laborers, compared to an average of just 3 percent for other immigrant groups. Those percentages remained nearly the same for the next twenty-five years. Irish men cleaned streets, dug ditches, toiled in mines, unloaded ships, and hauled bricks on construction sites. Women often worked as servants in private homes, where they were often abused and demeaned. Women also worked at home, sewing clothing for a dozen hours a day to earn just a few cents an hour.

▼ Workers cheer as the Central Pacific and Union Pacific Railroads meet to form the Transcontinental Railroad in Utah in 1869. Many thousands of Irish Americans labored to build the railroads.

Many Irish Americans worked in shops and factories making steel, tanning hides, butchering livestock, and producing cloth. These low-paying jobs were difficult and often dangerous because of a lack of safe conditions. It was common for workers to be burned while pouring molten steel.

Building the Railroad

In spite of discrimination, the hard work and bravery of Irish Americans shaped the United States in the 1800s. Between 1861 and 1865, for example, many thousands of Irish Americans fought in the Civil War. The construction of the Transcontinental Railroad, completed in 1869, would not have been possible without thousands of Irish Americans. They and other immigrants blasted tunnels through mountains, built bridges over gorges and rivers, and laid track across barren lands. The completion of the railroad had a huge impact on the growth of the country as settlers began to travel west in ever increasing numbers.

Children at School and Work

Teachers and students often discriminated against Irish American children who attended public schools. Because of the prejudice, and because Irish Americans wanted their children to have religious

Irish Americans in the Civil War

When the Civil War split the nation, Irish Americans fought on both sides of the conflict—an estimated 170,000 in the Union Army and about 40,000 with Confederate forces. More than 50,000 Union soldiers were born in Ireland, including some who joined as soon as their boats docked in the United States. They enlisted to get bonuses as high as $700 (about $14,000 today), a sum equal to ten years' wages in Ireland. Thomas McManus wrote home that "the bounty was very tempting and I enlisted the first day I came here."

▲ Brigadier General Michael Corcoran was commander of the Irish Legion, a combination of several regiments that fought on the Union side in the Civil War.

There were several all-Irish military units. The most famous was the Union Army's 69th New York State Volunteers, which became the nucleus of the Irish Brigade. The brigade's soldiers carried a flag into battle that represented Ireland—green with a golden harp, an Irish symbol. Catholic priests traveled with the brigade, holding religious services and praying for wounded soldiers. The Irish Brigade gained everlasting fame for the courage its soldiers displayed in battle. This glory came at a heavy price, however. After the Battle of Antietam in September 1862, Captain Michael O'Sullivan wrote: "Our brigade has been cut to pieces! Every man of my company has either been killed or wounded with the exception of eleven."

◀ An Irish American infantry regiment from Massachusetts poses for a photograph before celebrating mass in a Union Army camp in Virginia in 1861.

instruction, Catholic churches began opening their own schools in the late 1800s.

Many Irish American children, however, were forced to work to help their families survive. These young workers received little or no education because they could not go to school. Children as young as five years old sold newspapers, shined shoes, or worked in factories, doing whatever tasks they could handle.

"The machinery needed constant cleaning. The tiny, slender bodies of the little children crawled in and about under dangerous machinery, oiling and cleaning. Often their hands were crushed. A finger was snapped off. A father of two little girls worked a loom next to the one assigned to me. 'How old are the little girls?' I asked him. 'One is six years and ten days,' he said, pointing to a little girl, stoop-shouldered and thin chested, '[and] that one,' he pointed to a pair of thin legs like twigs, sticking out from under a rack of spindles, 'that one is seven and three months.' 'How long do they work?' 'From six in the evening till six comes morning.' 'How much do they get?' 'Ten cents a night.'"

Mary Harris "Mother" Jones, an Irish American who fought for workers' rights, describing working conditions in a textile factory in the mid-1800s

Living In Poverty

In the cities of the 1800s, Irish Americans were jammed into tiny apartments in large tenement buildings inhabited by hundreds of other poor people. Several families might share a single room in a tenement building that had no running water, a few outdoor toilets, and was poorly lit and ventilated.

▲ A group of textile mill workers in 1911 in Lowell, Massachusetts, includes several young boys. Irish American children started work at an early age to help support their families.

▲ In 1912, this typical tenement building in New York City contained small apartments crowded with immigrant families.
◄ An Irish American mother bathes her child in a small tin tub in a tenement apartment in about 1905.

"In Broad Street and all the surrounding neighborhood, including Fort Hill and the adjacent streets, the situation of the Irish is particularly wretched. . . . It is sufficient to say, that the whole district is a perfect hive of human beings, without comforts and mostly without common necessaries."

Health Committee report on living conditions, Boston, 1849

Tenements such as those that housed Irish immigrants were located in the poorest areas of each city. Garbage and other filth littered these poor neighborhoods, where deadly diseases—such as cholera, typhus, and tuberculosis—often spread fast through the buildings, killing many residents.

One of the largest Irish American neighborhoods in New York City was named "Hell's Kitchen" because so much violence and crime occurred there. Crushing poverty led many Irish immigrants to become criminals to survive. In Boston in the 1850s, half the people jailed for crimes were Irish American.

A high rate of alcoholism fueled the problems of poverty and crime that beset many Irish Americans in this period.

Remembering the Homeland

To help their communities and keep their ties to Ireland alive, Irish Americans of the 1800s started social and charitable organizations. The groups aided immigrants who were struggling to adapt to their new homeland as well as supporting the cause of Irish independence. The Ancient Order of Hibernians was one of the first such groups. By 1908, it had nearly two hundred thousand members.

In Ireland, the rural Irish had identified strongly with their village or county or clan. Like other immigrant groups in the United States, however, they found a new identity as a larger group—the Irish. Irish Americans sometimes greeted each other in Gaelic with "Erin Go Bragh," meaning "Ireland Forever." (Erin is another, more poetic name for Ireland.)

One way in which Irish Americans expressed their shared identity was to celebrate St. Patrick's Day every year on March 17. St. Patrick is the patron saint of Ireland because he introduced Christianity to the island. Irish Americans celebrated St. Patrick's Day for the first time in 1737 in Boston. The first parade took place in New York City in 1762. Over the years, St. Patrick's Day became an Irish American institution, marked with much more celebration and excitement than it had ever received in Ireland.

▲ Members of the Ancient Order of Hibernians, an Irish American society, received a certificate illustrated with many Irish symbols but topped with a U.S. flag.

"I can never forget home, as every Irishman in a foreign land can never forget the land he was raised in."

Maurice Woulfe, a soldier stationed at Fort Russsell, Wyoming, in a letter to his brother, 1870

Gaining Acceptance and Power

As a three-time mayor of Boston, governor of Massachusetts, and a U.S. Representative, James Michael Curley (1874–1958) was one of the twentieth century's most powerful Irish American political leaders. When asked why Irish Americans went into politics, Curley said they did it because it was "the quickest and easiest way for them out of the cellar."

▲ William R. Grace was born in County Cork in 1832. He made a fortune in shipping in North and South America and gave generously to help poor Irish and Irish Americans. He was elected mayor of New York City in 1880 and again in 1884.

Success in Politics

The long climb Irish Americans took to reach acceptance and a position of power started in the late 1800s. By then, there were several million Irish Americans, and they began to translate their growing numbers into power by voting in elections.

Irish Americans were encouraged to vote by politicians, mostly other Irish Americans. In 1880, William R. Grace was elected mayor of New York City, the first Irish Catholic to head a major U.S. city. Six years later, Hugh O'Brien became Boston's mayor. Both cities had large Irish American populations, and the key to the mayoral victories was that the Irish tended to vote as a group, which meant they did not dilute their voting power among several candidates. This political solidarity was born of Irish Americans' need to fight the discrimination they faced every day. In elections, almost all Irish Americans backed the Democratic Party because it was the party most willing to help struggling immigrants such as themselves.

> "My mother was obliged to work as a scrubwoman toiling nights in office buildings downtown. I thought of that one night while leaving City Hall during my first term as Mayor. I told the scrubwoman cleaning the corridors to get up: 'The only time a woman should go down on her knees is when she is praying to Almighty God,' I said. Next morning I ordered long-handled mops [and told] scrubwomen never again to get down on their knees in City Hall."
>
> *Mayor of Boston James Curley*

Government Jobs

Martin M. Lomasney, a son of poor Irish immigrants, became one of Boston's most powerful political figures in the early 1900s. He explained his key to political success: "I think that there's got to be in every ward somebody that any bloke can come to and get help." The Democratic Party made sure they had people in every ward who helped voters get jobs, housing, medical care, and even loans.

The most important benefit Irish Americans received from their new political power was better jobs. The congressmen, governors, and

Leading the Labor Movement

The discrimination Irish Americans faced in the 1800s made them realize the importance of decent jobs. As a result, many played an important role in establishing labor unions, which sought to improve wages and working conditions for all workers. In 1879, Terence Powderly, a son of Irish immigrants,

was elected head of the Knights of Labor. He helped the first large, national labor union grow to more than seven hundred thousand members. In the early 1900s, P. J. McGuire, another Irish American, cofounded the American Federation for Labor (AFL). By 1910, nearly half the AFL's members were Irish American; by 1920, the union had five million members. When the AFL merged in 1955 with the Congress of Industrial Organization (CIO), the first head of the AFL-CIO was George Meany, an Irish American. In 2005, the top leader of the AFL-CIO, the nation's largest union, was John Sweeney, another Irish American.

▲ Mary Harris "Mother" Jones traveled the United States for nearly fifty years, organizing strikes, supporting workers' rights, and campaigning against child labor.

mayors they elected showed their gratitude by making sure government agencies hired Irish Americans as teachers, clerks, policemen, and firefighters.

In the past, government officials had never hired Irish Catholics for such jobs, which paid more than unskilled work, were often easier to do, and gave workers more status in the community. When Michael Donohue immigrated to the United States in the early 1900s, he knew the best way to succeed was to secure a government job. "The only great desire I had was to become a civil servant," said Donohue, who became a New York City firefighter.

Skilled Workers

The growing political power of Irish Americans also led private businesses to stop discriminating against Irish Americans in hiring. By the early 1900s, the type of jobs Irish Americans held had changed drastically from a half-century earlier. No longer confined to digging ditches or pushing brooms, nearly 35 percent were working in businesses, 50 percent were skilled workers such as electricians, and only 15 percent remained unskilled laborers. Those percentages were similar among other immigrant groups, which meant Irish Americans had finally achieved job equality with other Americans.

New Opportunities

Better jobs allowed Irish Americans to earn more money, which helped them

◄ The Tammany Society, dominated by Irish Americans from the 1870s to the 1920s, controlled New York City politics for many years. The society's well known corruption was often represented by the Tammany Tiger, shown here in a theater poster from 1896.

improve their lives in other ways. Families moved out of tenement areas, such as Hell's Kitchen in New York City, to safer, cleaner neighborhoods and better apartments. As time went on, many Irish Americans were able to buy their own homes.

Freed from having to work to help support their families, children began attending school and even went to college. Many children attended Catholic schools that their churches started, and they later studied at Catholic universities, such as Georgetown and Notre Dame. Education allowed them to get better jobs as teachers, bankers, doctors, and lawyers.

The Irish Win Acceptance

Increased political power and improvement in their social status helped Irish Americans win

▶ Henry Ford (1863–1947) was the son of Irish immigrants who farmed in Michigan. He acquired immense wealth and power because of his skill in engineering and in business. Transforming U.S. industry with his assembly line technique, Ford became the nation's leading automobile manufacturer.

Irish Comic Strips

The first newspaper comic strip appeared in the *New York World* in 1895. It was called "Hogan's Alley," and it featured a strange-looking young man who was bald and always wore a yellow nightshirt. The comic strip became popular because of the funny antics of the youth, who was nicknamed the "Yellow Kid." His real name was Mickey Dugan, and he was clearly Irish American. Dugan lived in a rundown area populated by other strange, mostly poverty-stricken individuals. In 1913, a second comic strip featuring an Irish American appeared. The star of "Bringing Up Father" was Jiggs, a bricklayer who had suddenly become wealthy. The comic strip drew its humor from the problems Jiggs and his wife Maggie had in adapting to being rich. The differences between the two strips highlighted the economic progress of Irish Americans in U.S. society. When "Bringing Up Father" finally ended in 2000, it had become the longest-running daily comic strip in the world.

▲ An Irish American woman works building weapons in a Bren gun plant in 1942. Like all other Americans, Irish Americans contributed hugely to the U.S. war effort during World War II. Their hard work and patriotism were factors that overcame prejudice and led to acceptance.

acceptance from others. In 1916, the *Brooklyn Eagle* newspaper claimed that "the Irish have become an integral part of us, and even those of us who may have descended from the passengers of the *Mayflower* can hardly look upon them as foreigners." To compare Irish Americans to the settlers who had arrived in 1620 meant that they were finally considered full-fledged Americans.

This upward mobility is typified in the story of the Kennedy family. Patrick Kennedy was a poor Irish immigrant who came to the United States during the Great Famine. When Kennedy arrived in Boston, he made barrels and lived in a tenement. His son, Patrick Joseph, worked hard, saved his money, and bought a saloon. He became a successful businessman and then a political leader. Patrick Joseph Kennedy made enough money enough to send his son—Joseph P. Kennedy—to Harvard University. When Joseph P. Kennedy graduated, he became a banker and wealthy investor. When his son—John Fitzgerald—was born May 2, 1917, the Kennedy family was living in the fashionable Boston suburb of

Brookline. In just three generations, the Kennedys had transformed themselves from poor immigrants to powerful, wealthy, and prominent citizens.

Kennedy Triumphs

John Fitzgerald Kennedy would one day become president, but not before overcoming the anti-Catholic feeling that still lingered in the nation. Even though Irish Catholics had been gradually accepted into the mainstream of the United States, some people still rejected them because of their faith. In 1928, when New York governor Alfred E. Smith ran for president, he was defeated by Republican Herbert Hoover. Historians believe Smith lost partly because he was an Irish Catholic.

In his campaign for president in 1960, Kennedy dealt directly with questions about his religion. He won over Protestant voters by convincing them that his faith would not interfere with

"I am not the Catholic candidate for president. I am the Democratic Party's candidate for president who happens also to be a Catholic."

John F. Kennedy, in a campaign speech for the presidency, 1960

Two Irish American Presidents

In 1963, President John F. Kennedy visited Ireland, the land of his ancestors. When he addressed the Dail (the Irish national legislature), Kennedy noted that he was actually one of two Irish American presidents present. The other was Eamon De Valera, the president of Ireland. De Valera had been born in New York City on October 14, 1882, but when he was two years old, his Irish mother took him back to Ireland. De Valera grew up there and became an important figure in Ireland's successful fight to win independence from Britain. Kennedy told the Dail that, if his great-grandfather had not emigrated to the United States, he might have gone into politics and been elected to the Dail himself. He added, "Of course, if your own president had never left Brooklyn, he might be standing here instead of me."

the way he governed. His election as the nation's thirty-fifth president is considered a final victory over the ethnic and religious bigotry that had haunted Irish Americans for over a century.

Later Arrivals

As Irish Americans were gaining political power and acceptance, Irish immigration to the United States began to decline. The Irish who did arrive, however, had an easier time because they did not have to face the prejudice and discrimination that had greeted earlier immigrants. Mary Kenny immigrated to New York City in the 1960s. Soon afterward, she married Patrick Kenny, another immigrant, who became a successful stockbroker. The couple eventually became U.S. citizens and had three children. "We have been fortunate in America," said Mary Kenny. "This is the land of opportunity."

Patrick Fitzgerald emigrated in the late 1950s from County Clare. Although the only job he could get was as a hotel doorman, he was able to make a good life by working hard. He married Tillie, another Irish American, and on December 22, 1960, they had a son, also named Patrick. Their son went to Amherst College and then Harvard Law School. In 2005, he made headlines as a special prosecutor who investigated security leaks from the White House. Patrick Fitzgerald Jr. has been described as "an up-by-his-boot-straps Catholic boy with a strong sense of right and wrong." He believes his success is due to his parents: "I'm very indebted to my parents. They were very hardworking, straight, decent people."

The Irish are still coming to the United States, four hundred years after the first Irish immigrant landed in the colony of

◄ Irish Americans have always supported the cause of Irish independence. In the 1970s, these Irish American supporters of groups fighting British rule in Northern Ireland carried signs in a parade in Boston.

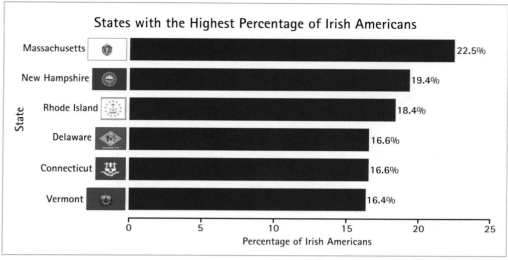

States with the Highest Percentage of Irish Americans

State	Percentage
Massachusetts	22.5%
New Hampshire	19.4%
Rhode Island	18.4%
Delaware	16.6%
Connecticut	16.6%
Vermont	16.4%

Percentage of Irish Americans

Source: U.S. Census Bureau, Census 2000

▲ Irish Americans live all over the United States, but Massachusetts, New Hampshire, and Rhode Island have the highest percentage of Irish Americans. The highest actual number of Irish Americans—more than 2,600,000 in 2000—live in California. The state of New York was close behind in 2000, with more than 2,450,000.

Jamestown, Virginia. From 2000 to 2004, more than fifty-five hundred immigrants arrived from Ireland.

The Irish Identity

Over the years, it became increasingly hard for many Irish Americans to hold on to their cultural identity. As many of them grew more affluent, they began leaving the tight-knit, poor Irish American neighborhoods in Boston, New York, Chicago, and Philadelphia. This migration away from Irish communities sped up after the end of World War II, when millions of people from all backgrounds began moving to the suburbs.

Although they were not isolated from other Irish Americans, these suburban dwellers were no longer surrounded by them nearly all the time. They became less likely to maintain Irish culture—by performing traditional songs or dances, for example, Irish foods, such as soda bread, became harder to find.

L. E. McCullough, the grandson of Irish immigrants, grew up in Indianapolis. "My family had become completely Americanized," he said. McCullough's Irishness was reborn in 1972, however, when he discovered Irish folk music. He began playing the flute and tin whistle, both traditional Irish instruments. Four years later, he won an all-Ireland competition, a rare feat for an American. McCullough also became a scholar of Irish music, hoping to hand down his knowledge to future generations of Irish Americans.

Irish Americans in U.S. Society

I n spite of their strong identity as U.S. citizens, descendants of Irish immigrants have maintained a loyal affection for their ancestral homeland. They also engage in many activities that demonstrate their pride in their Irish ancestry.

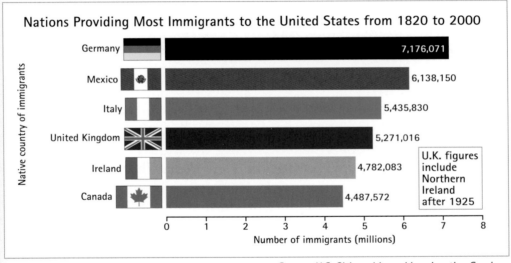

Nations Providing Most Immigrants to the United States from 1820 to 2000

Native country of immigrants

Country	Number
Germany	7,176,071
Mexico	6,138,150
Italy	5,435,830
United Kingdom	5,271,016
Ireland	4,782,083
Canada	4,487,572

U.K. figures include Northern Ireland after 1925

Number of immigrants (millions)

Source: U.S. Citizenship and Immigration Services

⏶ It is easy to see why Irish Americans have had such a huge impact on U.S. society. Between 1820 and 2000, Ireland was among the six nations providing the most immigrants to the United States.

Irish Heritage

Late Night television show host Conan O'Brien proudly claims, "I'm probably more pure Irish than people living in Ireland." His ancestors emigrated from Ireland during the Great Famine, and relatives on both sides of his family have always married other Irish Americans. O'Brien's family is in a minority, however. Most people today with Irish American heritage are not completely Irish.

Like other Americans, Irish Americans have, for generations, married people from different backgrounds and have a mixed heritage.

Since 1995, Congress has proclaimed March "Irish-American Heritage Month." Irish Americans lecture in schools about their culture and celebrate their heritage in events such as Irish Fest, held in Milwaukee, Wisconsin, each July. The world's largest Irish cultural festival, it showcases traditional dance, music, arts, and crafts. Similar festivals include the Indy Irish Fest in Indianapolis, Indiana, and the North Texas Irish Festival in Dallas, Texas.

Although it is estimated that fewer than thirty thousand Irish Americans speak Gaelic, many continue to learn traditional folk arts, such as step dancing. This dance form became popular in the 1990s thanks to Michael Flatley, who was born in Chicago to immigrant parents and says, "I'm proud of my Irish heritage." His shows created millions of new fans for Irish folk dancing.

In 2003, Irish Americans honored their heritage with the opening of the Irish Memorial in Philadelphia, Pennsylvania. Dedicated to

St. Patrick's Day

Celebrated on March 17, St. Patrick's Day continues to be the one day all Irish Americans honor their heritage. Cities with large Irish American populations—New York, Boston, and Chicago—hold parades. The city of Chicago even dyes part of its river green, in honor of the Emerald Isle. Americans in every city and of every heritage help Irish Americans celebrate St. Patrick's Day. They cheer at parades, eat corned beef and cabbage and Irish stew, and listen to traditional Irish ballads. St. Patrick's Day, more Irish American than Irish, has set a precedent for other U.S. holidays. Many immigrant groups, or their descendants, now take pride

in observing holidays that celebrate their heritage and give them an opportunity to share it with other Americans. In Ireland, meanwhile, the city of Dublin finally adopted this U.S. tradition in 1996, when Dubliners held their first St. Patrick's Day parade.

⌃ The section of the Chicago River that flows through downtown Chicago is dyed green for St. Patrick's Day.

the Irish who died during the Great Famine and those who fled from it, the memorial features a bronze sculpture of immigrants on a ship. Other famine memorials stand in Boston and New York City.

"The Irish Nation in America"

The legacy of Irish Americans is a rich one. In 2003, President George W. Bush praised the contributions they have made to the United States: "Americans of Irish descent have played a vital role in shaping our history and culture. America is a better nation because of the efforts of Irish Americans."

In addition to helping shape U.S. history, Irish Americans have made their mark on the United States in other ways. American country music is derived from Irish folk music, among other influences. So many U.S. communities bear Irish names that, in 1892, journalist John Deignan coined a term for them: "the Irish Nation

Leaders, Writers, and Entertainers

Americans of Irish descent have achieved success in every field of endeavor possible. Nineteen presidents and thousands of other political

leaders of Irish descent have led the United States. Henry Ford revolutionized transportation by introducing the first affordable automobile. In 1981, Sandra Day O'Connor became the first female U.S. Supreme Court justice. Playwright Eugene O'Neill and authors F. Scott Fitzgerald, Flannery O'Connor, Frank McCourt, and John O'Hara have greatly enriched U.S. literature. Georgia O'Keefe was a ground-breaking painter. James Cagney, John Wayne, Maureen O'Hara, Mickey Rourke, and Drew Barrymore have thrilled moviegoers, while Ed Sullivan, Mary Tyler Moore, Rosie O'Donnell, and Conan O'Brien have kept millions of viewers glued to their television sets. Across the nation, Americans have cheered on Irish American sports stars, such as boxers John L. Sullivan and Jack Dempsey, golfers Ben Hogan and Sam Snead, and tennis player John McEnroe.

▲ Ronald Reagan, the actor who became governor of California and president of the United States, was of Irish and Scotch-Irish ancestry.

in America." Dublin, California, is one of at least nine communities named after Ireland's capital. Shamrock, Texas; Emerald Isle, North Carolina; and Irish Channel, a neighborhood in New Orleans, all have names reflecting Irish American settlement.

Millions of Americans today eat corned beef and cabbage, a traditional Irish dish. They also use words that the Irish brought to the United States, such as *galore*, a Gaelic word that means enough. American sports fans cheer on the "Fighting Irish" sports teams of Notre Dame University and the Boston Celtics professional basketball team.

Irish and American

The fact that so much of Irish culture has become ingrained in U.S. society is due in part to the love Irish Americans have always had for Ireland. Despite that loyalty, most Irish immigrants have adopted U.S. citizenship. One of them is Pierce Brosnan, the movie actor who played secret agent James Bond. Brosnan grew up near Dublin and came to the United States in 1982. He became a U.S. citizen in October 2004. "I found a new life and identity in America," he said, "but my heart and soul will be forever Irish." The sentiment he voiced has been shared by millions of other Irish Americans who have found room in their hearts to love both nations.

▲ Many firefighters in New York City are of Irish descent, but as proud Americans, they carry U.S. flags in a St. Patrick's Day parade.

". . . the Irishman looks upon America as the refuge of his race, the home of his kindred, the heritage of his children and their children. . . . He has no feelings towards America but that of love and loyalty. To live on her soil, to work for the public good, and die in the country's service, are genuine aspirations of the son of Erin [Ireland], when he quits the place of his birth for that of his adoption."

Thomas Colley Grattan,
Irish travel writer who visited
the United States, 1859

Notable Irish Americans

John Barry (1745–1803) Irish-born naval hero of the American Revolution and first commander of the U.S. Navy.

Charles Carroll (1737–1832) colonial-born Irish Catholic land-owner and signer of the Declaration of Independence.

Davy Crockett (1786–1836) U.S.-born frontiersman and Congressman who died at the Battle of the Alamo in Texas.

Eamon De Valera (1882–1974) U.S.-born son of immigrants who returned to Ireland where he became a leader of Ireland's fight for inde-pendence and, from 1959 to 1973, the nation's president.

F. Scott Fitzgerald (1896–1940) U.S.-born son of Catholic Irish Americans, famous for his novels *This Side of Paradise* (1920) and *The Great Gatsby* (1925).

Henry Ford (1863–1947) U.S.-born son of Irish American farmers. He founded the Ford Motor Company and became the foremost U.S. pioneer of the automobile industry.

Andrew Jackson (1767–1845) colonial-born son of Scotch-Irish parents. He became a war hero and then (from 1829 to 1837) the first Irish American president of the United States.

Mary Harris Jones (1837–1930) Irish-born union organizer who helped found the Industrial Workers of the World in 1905 and organize strikes by the United Mine Workers.

John Fitzgerald Kennedy (1917–1963) U.S.-born descendant of a powerful Irish American Catholic family. He became the United States' first Catholic president.

Frank McCourt (1930–) U.S.-born son of immigrants who was raised in Ireland and remigrated to New York City, where he taught school, and became the prize-winning author of *Angela's Ashes* and other books.

Eugene O'Neill (1888–1953) U.S.-born Irish American who was the only U.S. playwright to win a Nobel Prize and is considered one of the greatest writers of the twentieth century.

Ronald Reagan (1911–2004) U.S.-born actor who became governor of California and then president of the United States (1981–1989) after a successful career as a movie actor.

Time Line

1171 England conquers Ireland.

1603 English seize Catholic land in Ireland's Ulster province and give it to Protestants, including the Scots whose descendants became the Scotch-Irish in America.

1607 First Irish immigrant arrives in North America.

1632 Catholic colony of Maryland is established.

1737 March 17: First St. Patrick's Day celebration in America is held in Boston, Massachusetts.

1762 First St. Patrick's Day Parade takes place, in New York City.

1775 Daniel Boone and several other Irish Americans found Boonesborough, the first white settlement in Kentucky.

1789 John Carroll is appointed first Catholic bishop of the United States.

1798 United Irishmen uprising fails to gain independence for Ireland.

1829 Scotch-Irish American Andrew Jackson becomes president.

1844 Nativists in Philadelphia destroy Catholic churches and kill thirteen Irish Americans.

1845 Great Famine begins in Ireland.

1855 Castle Garden immigration station opens in New York City.

1861 Civil War begins in the United States.

1869 Transcontinental Railroad is completed.

1879 Terence Powderly is elected head of Knights of Labor.

1880 W. R. Grace is elected mayor of New York City.

1892 Annie Moore from Ireland is the first immigrant to enter the United States through the Ellis Island immigration station.

1922 Irish Free State is created, slowing Irish emigration to the United States.

1949 Ireland becomes officially independent when the Republic of Ireland, or Eire, is declared. British parliament recognizes Ireland's independence.

1961 John F. Kennedy becomes the first Roman Catholic president of the United States.

1981 Ronald Reagan becomes president of the United States; Sandra Day O'Connor becomes the first woman to serve on the U.S. Supreme Court.

1995 Congress establishes Irish-American Heritage Month, now celebrated every March.

1997 Irish American author Frank McCourt wins the Pulitzer Prize for Biography for his childhood memoir *Angela's Ashes*.

2005 Americans exchange eight million St. Patrick's Day cards.

Glossary

blight plant disease that stops growth and causes crops to die

Celtic having to do with the Celts, tribes from Germany and France who dominated Europe from about 2000 B.C. to 400 B.C. Today, Gaelic-speaking people from parts of the British Isles, including Ireland and Scotland, are sometimes referred to as Celts.

civil servant person who works in a government job, including teachers, firefighters, police officers and other law enforcement workers, clerical workers, and tax officials

clan group of people or families with a common ancestor

colony nation, territory, or people under the control of another country

culture language, beliefs, customs, and ways of life shared by a group of people from the same region or nation

demean treat in a humiliating and degrading way

discriminate treat one group or person differently from another

emigrate leave one nation or region to go and live in another place

ethnic having certain racial, national, tribal, religious, or cultural origins

evict force people from their homes

famine period in which there is an extreme shortage of food

heritage something handed down from previous generations

Hibernian having to do with Ireland or Irish people

illiterate unable to read and write

immigrant person who arrives in a new nation or region to take up residence

indentured servitude condition in which a person is bound by an indenture, or contract of work, to be another person's servant for a period of time to pay off a debt

labor union organization, often in a particular trade or business, that represents the rights of workers

nativist person who wanted limits placed on U.S. immigration to protect the power and position of white, U.S.-born Americans

naturalization process of becoming a citizen by living in the United States for a number of years and passing a citizenship test

patron saint Catholic saints who are named as having special protective powers over a village, region, or aspect of life

prejudice bias against or dislike of a person or group because of race, nationality, or other factors

Protestant member of a non-Catholic Christian church, such as the Lutheran, Episcopalian, Methodist, or Presbyterian churches or the Church of England

steerage section of a steamship that provided poor accommodation and was used by passengers who could not afford cabins

tenement poorly built and crowded apartment buildings with bad ventilation and sanitation and low safety standards

ward district of a city when it is divided up into areas for voting and political representation

Further Resources

Books

Beller, Susan Provost. *Never Were Men So Brave: The Irish Brigade During the Civil War.* New York: Margaret K. McElderry, 1998.

Cooper, Ilene. *Jack: The Early Years of John F. Kennedy.* New York: Dutton Books, 2003.

Hoobler, Dorothy and Thomas Hoobler. *The Irish American Family Album.* American Family Albums (series). New York: Oxford University Press, 1995.

Hoobler, Dorothy and Thomas Hoobler. *We Are Americans: Voices of the Immigrant Experience.* New York: Scholastic, 2003.

Web Sites

American Foundation for Irish Heritage
www.irishamericanheritage.com
Web site of an organization that celebrates the contributions of Irish Americans

Immigration . . . Irish
memory.loc.gov/learn/features/immig/irish.html
Presentation about U.S. immigration from the Library of Congress

Ellis Island National Monument
www.nps.gov/elis
National Park Service information about Ellis Island

Publisher's note to educators and parents: Our editors have carefully reviewed these Web sites to ensure that they are suitable for children. Many Web sites change frequently, however, and we cannot guarantee that a site's future contents will continue to meet our high standards of quality and educational value. Be advised that children should be closely supervised whenever they access the Internet.

Where to Visit

The Irish Memorial at Penn's Landing
Front and Chestnut Streets
Philadelphia, PA 19106
Telephone: (215) 928-8801
www.irishmemorial.org

About the Author

Michael V. Uschan has written more than fifty books and has twice won the Council for Wisconsin Writers Juvenile Nonfiction Award. Uschan lives in Franklin, Wisconsin. His grandparents were all immigrants to the United States from Austria.

Index